THE
HONOR
of
YOUR
PRESENCE

McSWEENEY'S
SAN FRANCISCO

McSweeney's and colophon are registered trademarks of McSweeney's, an independent publisher based in San Francisco.

Cover illustration by Angel Chang.

ISBN 978-1-952119-90-3

10   9   8   7   6   5   4   3   2   1

www.mcsweeneys.net

Printed in Canada

THE HONOR of YOUR PRESENCE

DAVE EGGERS

McSWEENEY'S

HELEN HEARD A SWISH and a crackle from beyond her window, and knew her Uncle Peter had arrived. Always he showed up like this, like a restless child, racing to her house on a bicycle, dropping it carelessly into the juniper bush. He was sixty-two years old.

"Hellie?" he called.

"Back here," she answered, and saw his bald head glide past her lemon tree.

He opened the screen door and flew in. He was wearing madras shorts, an oversized polo shirt, and canvas boat shoes. The loose skin around his knees jiggled as he swept his eyes around Helen's office and finally collapsed on the futon. "Too hot out there to be biking," he said.

Helen regarded him. Uncle Peter was pale, pink, built like a tennis player, and covered in brown freckles. His chest was just short of concave, his back the slightest bit bent. He walked with a loping gait that brought to mind a shaggy hippie with no particular place to be.

"I don't know how you stand it out here in the middle of nowhere," he said. "Especially with you being so young and vibrant."

Helen did not usually consider herself so young and vibrant—she was thirty-one and had not exercised meaningfully in eighteen months—but she took the compliment, stored it away, knew she would visit it often.

She saw few people, and those she knew, professional acquaintances and distant cousins, were reserved and disinclined to make such pronouncements. She'd grown up in this town, Tres Pinos, between Killey Alley and Quien Sabes Road. It was scarcely a town, more of a stopover, but as soon as she could walk she'd found, among its few children, three friends, and they'd stayed together for the next few decades, a tight parallelogram of unquestioning loyalty. But in the last few years, they'd all moved away, Maria married and dragged to Connecticut, and Leonor gone to nursing school days before the pandemic. Helen was alone, in a suddenly silent world. Then came Peter.

Uncle Peter was known as a wild card, a character, a piece of work. He'd lived in London most of Helen's life, working in the theater as a stagehand and set painter, never accumulating family or wealth. For thirty-two years he'd rented a one-bedroom in Shoreditch, until Covid, when work dried up, his savings dwindled, and he'd spent his last thousand to come back to California. Like all things in the family, the reappearance of Peter Mahoney after three decades was treated with a shrug. Now he was living in Helen's garage in Tres Pinos, just inland and over the hills from Monterey in the oak-choked armpit between two parched yellow hills. He seemed perfectly content there. He had no material needs, it seemed. His only grievance was the heat.

"Yup, too hot for the bike," he said. Peter filled any silence with a reiteration, slightly altered, of whatever he'd just said.

"What're you working on?" he asked, and was instantly off the futon and at Helen's shoulder.

Helen was a designer specializing in event invitations of the high-end category. The brunt of her business was weddings, but she'd worked on fundraisers, galas, reunions, quinceañeras. The pandemic had flattened the business for the better part of two years, though the many false starts, almost-openings, had worked, oddly, in her favor. Clients ordered invitations, canceled, and ordered them again when the event was rescheduled. She discounted the second go-round, of course, but she had to charge something; her rates were already far lower than those of her competitors. She had steady work because she was on time, she was good—always good, not always great—and her overhead was low.

Overall, the purgatory of Covid had soured her on the industry—the gross expense of these gatherings, the largely fruitless pursuit of merriment and meaning. What if everything, permanently, were scaled back, or outright canceled? She mused this way daily. The towering stresses and exorbitant cost of these Babylonian weddings and fundraisers had gotten out of control. Maybe the pandemic was humbling us toward a more rational scale for our gatherings. Meet up with a few friends under a tree. Get married at City Hall and take a few pictures. Wasn't that enough? Parties were stressful, chaotic, invariably a lesser version of a dream. Things got broken, the food arrived cold, the music was too loud, the lead singer's outfit overshadowed the bride's. The invitations, on the other hand, could be perfect. They were inert, contained. They were the carefully-worded promise of a glorious event never realized.

"You ever go to any of these parties?" Peter picked up a finished invitation, embossed and with gilt edges.

"No," Helen said.

"But couldn't you just make an extra invitation?" Peter asked, and swept his hand toward her printer.

"First, this isn't where they're printed," Helen said, and explained the difference between a desktop inkjet printer and letterpress. That printing was done by a woman named Gwen, who worked out of a converted barn in San Ramon, a hundred miles northeast. Helen sent the digital files to Gwen, Gwen did the letterpress by hand, and then sent the finished invitations to the client. If the invitations or envelopes required calligraphy, that was done by a man named Guillermo, who lived even farther north, in a trio of trailers on the mohair shores of Lake Berryessa. And everything started with Sona, the event coordinator who sent them all business. She was legendary—detail-obsessed, uncompromising, and the most miserable person any of them knew.

"So how do *you* get copies?" Peter asked, and nodded at Helen's wall, where invitations to past events were pinned.

"Gwen always prints a few extras for me."

Peter gave her an imploring look.

"I'm not going to a wedding I'm not invited to," Helen said. "Sona would fire me in a second."

"Not a *wedding*," Peter said. "But what about that one?" He pointed to an invitation to the Monterey Bay Aquarium's summer fundraiser, The Big Splash. "There must be a thousand people going. No one would notice us."

"No," Helen said. "And not with you."

"I could die any day. You should take me," he said.

"You're not sick. Are you sick?"

Staring at her sweating, wild-eyed uncle, Helen realized she knew very little about him. She had five uncles on her mother's side alone, and these uncles had begat at least thirty cousins. Peter, this London uncle, *could* be dying. The way information flowed in their family—sporadic, incomplete, unreliable—he or anyone could have days to live and she wouldn't know it.

"Did I tell you about my friend who died of an aneurysm?" he asked.

"The guy at the tire shop in town?" Helen asked.

For some reason, Peter had befriended a man named Gus, the second-in-command at the local tire store. Pudgy, boyish, and mostly bald, he was anywhere between thirty-five and fifty. Wherever Helen saw him, he looked happy, eager, wholly content, like a boy lined up at the ice cream truck, money in hand. Gus came around Peter's garage every Sunday morning and stayed till 10 p.m., the two of them sitting in the dappled shade of the live oaks, drinking spiked lemonade. What they talked about for twelve hours at a stretch was an unsolvable enigma.

"No. That's Gus," Peter said, and dropped himself back onto the futon. "Gus had a stroke, but he's fine. The guy who died of the aneurysm really died. He was exactly my age."

"Sixty-two."

"Well, this was four years ago. So fifty-eight. Quite sobering."

"So now you've vowed to go to parties to which you're not invited."

"Not specifically, no. But it's the kind of opportunity we'd both be mad to pass up."

Mad was one of Peter's few Britishisms. In thirty years in London, he'd picked up *mad* to supplant the American *crazy*, and he sometimes *fancied* things. Otherwise, there was almost no evidence he'd been gone so long.

"So I assume it's a go?" he said. Peter clasped his freckled hands behind his head. Gangly and constantly moving, wherever he was, Peter seemed at once ill at ease and absolutely comfortable in his skin.

"No," Helen said, and went back to her screen, hoping he'd take the cue and leave. And maybe take a shower. She'd been picking up on a ripe smell in the room and now realized it was him. Peter stood again and hovered over her shoulder. The odor was fruity, acidic. She held her breath, and he moved back to the wall of proofs.

"Too many of my friends have died," he said. He unpinned the Big Splash invitation and held it like a reliquary. "And it's a costume party! This can be something we look forward to," he said, running his aristocratic fingers over the thick board, its deep embossing. "Something extraordinary to do in a short life."

Peter found a folding chair and arranged it next to Helen.

"Helen," he said, looking at every part of her face and hair. In the noonday light, his blue eyes were incandescent. "Your problem is that you spread word of celebrations, without getting to join in."

"That's not my problem," she answered. Her problem, the one that had preoccupied her for months, was that her house was on septic, and the septic tank was under the house, and the tank was full.

"You spend too much time alone," he said. "I don't want you to have regrets. I have so many. So many things I'd do differently."

She'd never seen him look so serious.

"You're not serious," she said.

"No, I'm not serious," he laughed, and his face burst open. "I'm not serious, no. But the reason I don't have regrets is because I took advantage of stuff like this. Fun stuff where no one's harmed."

"I think you're bored out here in the hills," she said. "Maybe you should go to the city." She was thinking of San Francisco, but he thought of London.

"I'm not ready to go back," he said. "But out here, yes, in Tres Pinos I am absolutely bored. And it's so hot. Let's go over the mountains and to the sea."

Peter ordered the costumes from an Etsy person, using Helen's credit card, and thanked Helen profusely for covering the cost. He'd ordered a leopard seal for himself, a whale-shark for Helen.

Now, on a gusty gray Monterey afternoon, they were parked a quarter-mile from the aquarium, standing on the road's gravel shoulder, changing. She was miserable. Peter was giddy. Beyond her was the Pacific, pale and frothing.

Somehow she didn't think any of this would actually happen—that the costumes would arrive, that they'd actually get in the car and drive an hour to sneak into a gala. Now she regretted not thinking harder about the marine mammal she'd chosen. The costume was enormous.

"I'll be knocking over trays and glasses all night," she said, seeing her vast reflection in the window of her Nissan.

"I bet it's warm in there," he said, meaning inside her costume, which was made of synthetic material Helen was certain wouldn't breathe, and was likely flammable.

Peter was bent over, twisting his feet through his costume, which was lean and convincing.

"Why is yours so much better than mine?" she asked.

"Yours is great! Can you walk?" he asked. She waddled along the road.

"Perfect," he said. "You said you wanted your face hidden. It's definitely hidden."

That had been the first of the demands she'd made. They would not eat or drink at the event, either, she insisted; that would be stealing. The third demand was that they would endeavor to be quiet and invisible, and would leave the moment anything felt strange for them or their hosts.

"Yup, your face is impossible to see," he said.

Now dressed, Peter made for the museum without looking back. He had a way of drifting away, chin aloft, from whomever he was with. Years ago, at the funeral of his own mother, Helen's grandmother, he'd walked away from the burial—during the burial—hands behind his back, reading other gravestones. At the reception afterward, he praised the ceremony as glorious, dignified, perfect—as if no one had seen him leave.

They approached the museum's entrance. She was already soaked in sweat. Outside, dozens of adults and children were gathered, all dressed as fish and dolphins and sea captains. There was a family of penguins, the last of which was no bigger than a bowling pin.

"Will you wait a second?" Helen asked. He stopped. She waddled to him.

"What will you say if someone asks why you're there?"

"I'm rich and I love fish," he said.

"Don't say that, please," she said. "Don't say anything memorable or funny."

"Nothing memorable or funny, got it," he said.

"If I'm found out," she said, "I'll never work again. Sona might even be there." Helen didn't think this was true, that her boss would attend such a thing, but now it seemed a grave possibility. She wanted badly to go home. Helen never went where she was not invited. Not in high school, not in college, not ever.

"We're fine," Peter said. "No one can possibly see you."

"Don't talk to anyone," Helen said. "I know how chatty you are."

Peter made a mouth-zipping gesture with a spotted fin, and got in line behind the bowling-pin penguin. By shifting her head left and right, Helen could make out the greeters just outside the aquarium entrance. They were two young women in crisp white dress shirts, black pants and sky-blue Covid masks. Each held a tablet and seemed to be checking the guests against the list.

"We're not on the list," Helen said.

"The paper invite will work," Peter said. "Only a real guest would have one."

Helen's thighs were sweating.

"You have ours?" Peter asked.

Helen could feel the oversized, cardstock invitation in her waistband. With no pockets big enough to hold it, she'd stuck it between her pants and stomach. Her right hand retreated from the fin and, in the costume's vast hollow, she grabbed the invitation and pushed it up through the costume's mouth, where she retrieved it with her left fin.

Peter took it, and they moved toward the door, finding themselves behind a tall man dressed as a hammerhead. He entered without incident, and when it was their turn, one of the greeters took the invitation from Peter's fin and said, "Welcome," without even glancing at it.

"Told you," Peter said.

Outside it had been cold and gray, but inside there was amber light from Chinese lanterns, Lizzo's "Water Me" blasting through the grand atrium, and a bearded waiter was offering them champagne.

"Yup, I told you," Peter said, and then was gone. Not gone, but going. She caught his silky, spotted shape, chin up, meandering into the crowd as if summoned.

Helen waddled toward the bearded waiter and asked for a glass. He offered her his tray, she took a flute and looked for somewhere to sit. She could make it through any social predicament as long as she was sitting. She found a padded bench and slowly lowered herself until her costume billowed out in front of her. Now her face was deeper in shadow, and she felt like she was both within the party and watching from some misshapen closet.

She sipped on her champagne and took it all in. There were children everywhere—hundreds of them. She had not expected children. They were dressed as dolphins and orcas and squids, and there was a small dance floor, where three adolescent girls in jellyfish costumes were twisting before the DJ, a teenager dressed as a manatee. Next to him was another man, disguised as a mid-century sailor, with a scarf and bellbottoms.

"Vegan pasta puffs."

A different waiter was standing over her. Helen extended her hand through the whale-shark mouth and took two pasta puffs and a napkin.

"Thank you," she said. "What's that?" the waiter said.

She pictured herself at the bottom of a well, screaming to be heard. "Thank you!" she yelled, and the waiter smiled and spun off.

Another waiter followed with more champagne; she took a fresh glass. For years Helen believed events like this would be insufferable, bizarrely counter-productive. Why not use all the money spent on the event to fund the actual cause? Sona had explained the spend-money-to-make-money concept to her, but Helen remained unconvinced. Still, this was fun. It was unpretentious, like an oversized multigenerational birthday party. There was a coloring station, and a shallow pool where guests could touch mollusks and skates, and there was a kind of laboratory for the making of exotic marine-themed cocktails. But where was Peter? She turned and heard a crash.

Her tail had knocked a plate off her bench. She maneuvered her head-hole until she saw that she'd sent it hurtling ten yards into the lobby. But the plate was plastic, and hadn't had food on it, and it was quickly gathered up by a passing waitress. Every bit of contentment she'd felt moments before turned to sour self-loathing. Helen had always been tall and awkward in her body; her mother had promised grace would come, but grace had not come. She needed to leave. Or half-leave. To go outside.

She rose, steadied herself, planning to find her way to the deck. *Shit*, she hissed from her hollow. She was already tipsy. She should have eaten dinner. Costume tipsy was different than everyday tipsy. *Shit, shit*. She walked slowly through the main room, trying to make her languorous pace true to a whale-shark. Weren't they slow? They were! They were! She stepped steadily, as in a procession of one. All the while she stayed close to the perimeter, running her fins along the surface of walls and columns until she came upon the dance floor. Its minefield of flailing bodies was just before the door to the deck; she only had to get across without knocking over an adolescent jellyfish-girl.

"You okay?" a voice said.

She turned suddenly, thrusting her snout into the head of the mid-century sailor. "Sorry!" she said, and from the darkness of her cavern tried to ascertain the damage to him. While finding him unharmed, she saw a Polish flag on his shoulder. But did Poland *have* a navy?

"Not a problem," he said, and shook his face theatrically, like a boxer recovering from a sucker punch. He was a beautiful thing, with huge brown eyes and a delicate jaw. She expected him to quickly move away, but he lingered.

"Are these girls digging your dance moves, sailor?" Helen said. She customarily, reflexively, said aggressive things to handsome men.

His face registered real surprise, then outrage, as if the full weight of the false accusation had finally landed. "I'm the party starter," he said. "This is my *job*."

Helen's face burned, and she cursed her terrible mind and horrible mouth. She yelled another "Sorry" from the depths of her disguise, and then waddled to the back door and burst through to the deck. In the ocean air she found her way to the redwood railing and collapsed against it. Once every year or two, she encountered someone she found alluring, and her mouth spewed bile. How could she remember not to do something like that, given it only happened once every few years? And wasn't it natural enough—the spouting of hateful banter at a perfect and friendly face? She was out of practice, had been out of practice for the better part of a decade.

Helen had only truly adored one person, and that had been a mistake, a small-town mistake obvious to all but her. How stupid to fall for Maria's brother? He was four years older, and she and Leonor had grown up seeing him as the unassuming, unattainable model of masculinity. But then he'd returned from college, and when she was eighteen, he made himself suddenly attainable—to Helen. For a summer they acted on ten years of latent desire, in a private frenzy, most of it outdoors. Then she went to college downstate, he took a job in Dubai, and he never looked back.

She thought he might look back, and for years she was ready for him to look back, but he never turned around.

From the safety of her cave-mouth, she peeked through the glass and at the dance floor, to see how the Polish sailor was faring. He was back to party-starting, bouncing up and down with a toddler on his shoulders.

"Fuck, this is wonderful," Peter said. He had sidled up next to her. His flippers were on the wooden railing. "Don't you think?"

"I'm on the fence," she said. It took him a second to get the joke.

He lifted his seal-snout. "Hellie, don't you *long*?"

"Don't I long?" she asked, looking at a seagull eating someone's forgotten sushi, jabbing at it on the wet, blue deck.

"Don't you *long*?" he asked again, stretching the word out this time and giving it a guttural edge. His eyes met hers in a kind of challenge.

"Yes," she said. "Sure. All the time. Did it this morning."

"You have to long for *some*thing," he said, looking straight down to the inky sea. "Longing is such pleasure. It's like chocolate and cannabis in a hot tub—only you don't have any of those things. It's *wanting* all those things, and also wanting meaning, and love, and the sense that you're on a reckless adventure, seeing things that have never been seen."

"Okay," she said. She really didn't know this man. Was he about to confess something to her? He was gay, she assumed, but this had never been said. Maybe he was bi?

"Hellie, I want to know what you long for," he said. He took her fat gray fin in his flipper and looked at it.

A rush of thoughts came to Helen. She actually had an answer. Just a few days ago, while sleeping through the first bright hours of morning, she'd had a vivid dream (all her most vivid dreams were in the morning). In it, she was lying on a bed, high in the air. The bed was on a kind of pedestal, forty feet up, in the middle of a meadow, and outside it was night, a gauzy lavender night, and the stars and planets were out, and there was someone next to her who was soft and gentle and radiating love and giddiness, and the face was smiling, eyes delighted. It seemed a woman's face, but that's all she knew.

Helen wanted to tell him this, but before she could, he spotted the champagne glass in her other fin. It was near-empty.

"You broke your rule!" he said. "You said we couldn't eat or drink. I'll be right back." And he was off, headed to the outdoor bar at the end of the deck.

Helen was alone again, and anonymous, and aglow with champagne and a handful of crackers and carrots she'd taken into her mouth-cavern. She walked back inside, and moved slowly, dreamily, through the galleries of bright blue glass, where barracudas, belugas, sailfish and turtles moved like dazed tourists in their crowded tanks. After an hour she found herself among a small group of guests watching a magician do impossible tricks at close range. He was not in costume, but in all black—black pants, black shirt, black vest, black beard.

He was engaged with a silver-haired man in an admiral's outfit. After some banter, the magician pulled a gold coin from his own mouth, and this gold coin had on it the name of the silver-haired man standing before him.

"That's the most astounding thing I've ever seen," the silver-haired man said. "And I own a professional hockey team." As he and the magician talked about hockey and close magic, a regal woman of about sixty, dressed as a scaly sea-goddess, took notice of Helen.

"Are you here alone, hon?" she asked. Helen assumed she was the hockey man's wife. As their eyes met, her stare hardened from sympathetic to suspicious.

"No, my uncle's here somewhere," Helen mumbled, and her thighs began to sweat again. She looked intensely into the aquarium, as if he might swim by.

"Your uncle, do we know him?" the sea-goddess asked, fingering a glittering necklace. Her eyes were ice-blue, her fingers like pink talons. Helen was certain the sea goddess knew she was uninvited. This was why she didn't come to these things—this feeling of not being fully welcome. Everywhere, there were levels of welcome, and the owner of the hockey team, whose name was on the coin in the magician's mouth, was at the top, his sea goddess at his side. And they looked down to the muddy ocean floor to see Helen, hiding in her mouth-cavern.

"You probably know him," Helen said. "He owns a hockey team, too. Isn't that weird? Field hockey, but still. Let me go get him."

She took the stairs recklessly and found refuge near a tall aquarium full of jellyfish, falling like snow. Something brushed the back of her leg, and she turned to find an enormous octopus, seven feet high and with all eight tentacles, gliding by. The person inside was wholly hidden, even their legs, and the effect was so magical that Helen felt a tingling rush of gratitude; people went to such lengths to make something like that, some beautiful and useless deception.

Just as the octopus turned a rounded corner, the Polish sailor emerged from a nearby bathroom, checking his zipper. Finding it satisfactory, he looked up and saw Helen. In three quick strides he was standing close, his face made more extraordinary in the soft peach light of the jellyfish tank.

"I wasn't dancing with the kids for *fun*," he said. "It's my *job*," he said again.

"I know, I know!" Helen said, and pelted him with clumsy apologies for the next few minutes. Finally he softened.

"I'm Bartek. Are you here alone?" he asked. He was half-Polish, and his grandfather was actual-Polish, he said, and the uniform he wore was his grandfather's. He touched the medals on his chest, declaring them real. She found this unaccountably sexy, and brought her face closer to the whale-mouth, hoping Bartek might see her eyes smiling at him.

She told Bartek about Uncle Peter, mentioning his habit of abandoning her, in hopes that Bartek might feel, out of chivalry, an obligation to stay with her. She didn't know if his party-starting was finished—did someone else finish what he had started? Was there a party-ender? Because she knew the event ended at nine, and that soon she'd have to take a drunken Peter home, she only wanted to glean some knowledge about Bartek that would ensure she could find him again.

"I live up in Redding, actually," he said, "but I'm working at a thing in Gilroy next weekend. I think it's open to the public. Maybe you should come."

Again her mouth tried to say something terrible to him, something nasty about Gilroy, but this time she fought the impulse and said she would try.

He provided the details, and the lights dimmed and then went horrifically bright, indicating the night was over. Peter arrived, drunker than Helen thought possible, holding an ice-cream sandwich in his leopard-seal fin. Seeing the Polish sailor up close, Peter saluted, slurred a few words of greeting in a newfound British accent, and Bartek, sober and tired, excused himself and spun away.

On the way home, Peter kept his head out the window, grinning into the wind like a dog. "Everything about that was worth it," he yelled.

In the past, after Helen had attended any social event where she'd had alcohol and spoken words to people, she'd spend weeks lamenting every catty or ignorant thing she'd said, every clumsy walk to and from the bathroom, every person she'd kissed in the lobby while the overnight janitor polished the floors with a spinning green machine. And it had all gotten far worse when her friends left town. There was no one to reassure her she had not behaved like an idiot.

But after the party in Monterey, no such regrets had haunted her. Her name had not been known, her face was hidden, she could not possibly get caught or face consequences. She could move freely and see all and go home, and only she knew it had happened. It was invisibility and flight. She was entertaining the possibility of a long public life dressed as a whale-shark when she heard the shush of Peter's bicycle landing in her juniper.

"Hellie?" he called out.

His bald head sped past her lemon tree and appeared, with the rest of him, in her office.

"So," he said, as he studied her wall, where six new proofs were taped. "Anything good coming up?"

"No," she said. She had not ruled out going to another event, but had ruled out going with Peter. He was too careless, and he vastly increased the risk of discovery. But she had decided not to tell him this, or about the Gilroy event, which she'd been considering attending.

"What about this one?" he asked. He pointed to an invitation to a corporate event in San Jose. His eyes darted over the page. "It's an afternoon thing for the whole family," he said. "And Billy Idol's playing! Don't you want to see Billy Idol?"

She did want to see Billy Idol.

"No," she said.

"Did I ever tell you I know his nephew? He was a lighting tech in London. He had a goiter, which I thought unusual."

Peter had pulled the invitation off the wall.

"Don't," Helen said. "They have a guest list for that one. And each invite has the person's name done by a calligrapher. There's no way to sneak in."

"Is this the list?" Peter asked. He'd found the printout on her worktable. Sona had sent it to her, and Helen was supposed to send it to the calligrapher.

"Why not just add me to this?" he asked.

"You know I can't do that."

"Did you get this digitally?" Peter asked.

"Yes," she said.

"So just add me and print it out again. My last name's different than yours. No one could possibly connect this to you. You add my name to this list on your computer, you print it out again, you send it to the calligrapher. Easy."

"No."

"You can be my plus one."

"The event is too small," Helen said.

"It doesn't look small," Peter said. "It says it's at a fairgrounds. You can't have a small event at a fairgrounds. Can you ask Gwen how many invites she's printing?"

"How do you know about Gwen?"

"You told me about her. Your letterpress friend."

"Well, she's not my friend. I've never met her," Helen said.

"You've never met her? How often do you get out socially, Hellie?"

Helen said nothing. He knew she never went out. They saw each other, heard each other, every day in their armpit-valley.

"Sorry. That was out of bounds," he said. "I just thought we had fun last time. Didn't we?"

"It was fine," she said.

"Fine. Okay. And this one's outside, and it's Billy Idol. Far more casual. It's like sneaking into a county fair. No one cares."

They did not go to Billy Idol. But the only way to get Peter off her back about Billy Idol was to take him to Gilroy, where Bartek's next gig would be. The Gilroy Garlic Festival had an opening-night party, and this seemed an easy compromise.

But she couldn't be complicit. She needed some measure of plausible deniability, so she had looked away from her keyboard and let Peter type his name onto the calligrapher's list. Somehow it mitigated her guilt, and he'd gotten his invite in the mail like anyone else. She was just his plus one. It was all absurd, but she was as invisible as before, and now they were pulling off the highway to enter Gilroy.

"You have the invite?" she asked.

Peter held it up. It had been beautifully hand-written by Guillermo, but seeing Peter's name on that envelope turned her stomach. Printing an extra invite was one thing; this was a more florid kind of fraud.

The late afternoon heat was still coming off the pavement. Growing up in Tres Pinos, Helen thought of Gilroy as the big city—the place everyone wanted to leave Tres Pinos for. She hadn't been there in years, and now half the town's businesses were dead by Covid, boarded up.

"I don't remember this place," Peter said. "And I don't smell the garlic. Did it ever smell of garlic?"

It did, often, smell of garlic. And to compensate, someone, a hundred years ago, decided to embrace it—to make Gilroy the Garlic Capital of the World. It was on every sign, every T-shirt, and they'd made the harvest a time of citywide celebration. The opening gala was being held at the Ramada, and when they pulled into the lot, older adults in bright cowboy costumes wound their way through trucks and SUVs, heading toward the Ramada's cul-de-sac. A new surge of Covid was blasting through the region, so guests had been asked to wear masks, and were encouraged to wear bandanas over the masks. *Let's Make this Outlaw!* the email update pleaded.

"Can you do mine?" Peter asked. He handed her his bandana, black with gold lacing. She tied it on, and she turned to let him fix hers. Knowing only her eyes would be visible to Bartek, she'd

45

spent an hour on them, using far more eyeliner and mascara than she'd ever dared before.

"Liz Taylor!" Peter said.

"It's not too much?" she asked.

"No. And I like the pants. Sorta seventies-country. Very East End, 1983."

Helen did not know what that meant, but took it to mean something British. She'd found, online, a pair of silky royal-blue pants with white Western stitching. They were tight in the thighs, loose at the ankles, and made in Serbia.

"Now can I do something?" he asked.

Flush from his compliments, she agreed.

"Your posture is shit," he said, and her confidence shattered.

He stood at her side and pulled her shoulders back, squinting. Wanting to curse him and run, she only managed a breathless grunt.

"Better!" He stepped back. "Chin straight," he said, and inched her chin up with his knuckle.

All this in the parking lot. Helen looked around. No one was watching.

"*So* much better," he said.

"I don't stoop," she said. People thought she stooped, had been saying this since she was thirteen. Her mother had long ago given up the fight.

"Not anymore you don't," he said. "I know you were tall as a girl, but you're not so tall now. Five-nine?"

"About." She was five-ten and a half.

"There was an actress in London," Peter said, "you know her now, but I knew her when she was just out of Royal Shakespeare. She was six foot barefoot and hunched a bit, like you. The director insisted she stand straight up. She was playing Medea—definitely a tall woman's part.

She straightened up and my god, she was like a Corinthian column."

"I don't want to be a Corinthian column," she said.

"I know. But Medea? Let's see you walk like Medea," he said.

"No," Helen said. She didn't know how Medea walked, and she was finished with all this. "Can we just go inside?"

"We can," he said, and he was at the door of the Ramada in seconds, leaving her far behind. Peter was wearing black jeans and a brown suede shirt with black stitching. He'd borrowed it from Gus, and looked fully the part of a working farmhand cleaned up for a night in town. She caught up with him at the doorway, where a pair of women in their seventies were sitting on high wooden stools.

"Hello, handsome!" one said.

"Hello, gorgeous!" Peter said. The British accent was back in force. He handed the invitation to the woman, who didn't look at it. She waved them through.

"All that work, all that intrigue," Helen said.

"We are but dust," Peter said.

The room was beige and sterile, lightly decorated by what appeared to be four different people trying to evoke four different eras. The large garlic cutouts on the walls looked vaginal, the flowers on the tables were dried but not yet dead, there were six ice sculptures of dubious stability, and the waitstaff looked like casino dealers—in black formalwear with red ties.

The hundred or so guests were huddled by the walls or milling around the tables where raffle items were offered. On the opposite corner of the ballroom was a sorry dancefloor, and in the middle of it, Bartek. Helen had to assume it was Bartek. In a white Stetson and sky-blue jeans, the figure he cut was wholly different than at the aquarium. In that costume, he'd been masculine and convincing—a meat-eating exemplar of a remorseless superpower. Tonight he looked like a Branson backup dancer.

"Hello young lady," he said, loudly. There was something performative and general in his voice that strongly implied that he didn't recognize her.

"Bartek," she said. His look was blank. "It's Helen. We met at the aquarium."

"The aquarium?" He looked around, as if he'd find one there, in the ballroom.

"In Monterey. By the jellyfish. I was a whale—"

"Oh!" he yelled. "Yes, I know!" Now he knew. Did he really know? "You came!" he said, slightly less loud now. He was wearing a red bandana over an N95. "Do you live here in Gilroy?" he asked, while looking over her shoulder. Two women had just entered the ballroom, one of them holding a clipboard.

"Stay here," he said. "I'll be right back."

There had been no recognition, no spark. Screw it. Bartek was a bust. Helen was ready to leave. During Covid you could leave moments after arriving and no one could question it. Everyone was ghosting, canceling, not bothering. It was a pandemic well-suited to her natural inclinations.

She looked around the room for her uncle. He was standing at the raffle table with a soft-bellied man about his age. They were inspecting one of the offerings, a week at a ski-in house in Tahoe.

"Do you ski?" she asked, and Peter practically jumped, his eyes white. The man next to him turned, too, and Helen realized it was Gus, his friend from the tire shop. He had a suede cowboy hat by his side. He put it on and tipped it to her.

"Hi Gus," she said.

"Hi Helen," he said.

"You paid to go to this?" she asked.

Gus looked at Peter, who looked at the ceiling. Finally she put it together.

"You put him on the list, too," she said.

Peter was not apologetic. If anything, he seemed to be blaming Helen. Of course he would abuse the moment she'd given him at her keyboard.

"Don't worry," he said. "Gus won't tell."

Gus crossed his heart with his pudgy finger.

"I'm leaving," she said.

"I'm staying," Peter said. "We drove an hour."

She walked away, now truly wanting to exit,

but then found two things she wanted in one place: the bar, and Bartek. He was talking to the bartender, a woman of about forty wearing a tight Western shirt the color of butter.

A couple was at the bar, complaining loudly about the cost of their babysitter, dinner for the babysitter, then their Uber and dinner before the event. "All for this!" the woman, a slinky blonde, said, and swept her hand around the joyless room.

"There's just no point," the man said under his fake handlebar mustache.

They left, and Bartek stared daggers at their retreat.

"Sauv blanc, please," Helen said to the bartender, who seemed wholly unaffected by the couple's bleating.

"Sure, sweetie," the woman said.

Helen had a weakness for terms of casual endearment like this. The women who used them had to be warm, confident, loving. What a gift, to be able to pull off a *sweetie* with a stranger.

She lifted her chin to Bartek. "Ready to party-start?"

Again he looked at Helen as if he'd never seen her before, so she took a long pull on her wine and turned toward the bartender. The woman's hair was reddish, probably dyed, pulled back into a ponytail. Her face was round, cheeks rosy, and that chest—it was enormous.

"I think so," Bartek said. "How about you?"

He still had no idea who Helen was.

"Am *I* ready to party-start?" she asked.

He nodded, looked beyond her, then back at her. He smiled politely, clearly accustomed to

talking to drunken strangers who wanted their
songs played, who wanted to stomp around to
"Come On Eileen" at their high school reunion.

"This is a tough crowd," he said, and eyed the
empty dancefloor as a general would a battlefield.
"Kids make it easier. I think you're the youngest
person here."

He glanced her way, studying her briefly. Still
nothing.

"Well, I better go," Bartek said, and made a
quick diagonal across the ballroom to his post.

The busty bartender had refilled Helen's glass
already, a generous second pour, and had added
a pink napkin around the stem. Bartek had left
without a drink, and by this Helen assumed that
he'd been visiting the bar for the bartender, not
a beverage. Helen wilted. She could not compete
with a pretty, shapely person like this, a woman

with the curves of a fertility idol and the sunny manner of a kindergarten teacher.

"Thanks," she said to her, and looked for somewhere to sit. In the corner of the ballroom, she saw a zigzag row of folding chairs, and next to it, an abandoned wheelchair.

"You bet, hon," the bartender said, and held her gaze for a moment just longer than casual.

Helen shuffled away and sat on the chair farthest from the wheelchair. She sipped her sauv blanc and stole a few glances toward the bartender, who was by then surrounded by a group of elderly drinkers. The room filled until a hundred or so were wandering unhappily between the bar and the raffle table. It was a truly terrible party. There was too much space, too much floor.

"Hey hey party people!" Bartek said from his microphone, and encouraged the attendees to

gather near the stage. "No stampeding, please,"
he added, and laughed to himself for an inordi-
nately long time. A woman introduced herself
as the deputy mayor and made solemn remarks
about garlic, and then introduced a succession of
board members past and present. The last speak-
er cued Bartek, who began with "Billie Jean,"
which had no takers. "September Song" had no
effect. Helen returned to her conclusion that
most gatherings were horrific wastes of time and
money and goodwill.

She couldn't find Peter and Gus. Maybe
they'd left. Bartek was likely going home with
the big-pour bartender, and Helen was happy for
them. They were in the same industry, making do
with an insufferable species that tried in vain to
have fun. Even if she had to wait in the car for an
hour or two, she had to leave this room. Heading

toward the exit, Helen glanced back at Bartek and his tragic dance floor, and saw a man on all fours.

At first she assumed one of the septuagenarians had fallen, but then another man—oh god, it was Peter—came out of nowhere and leap-frogged over the man on all-fours, who of course was Gus.

Helen couldn't watch, couldn't look away. She stood in the middle of the ballroom, mouth agape. Gus got up from the floor, and he and Peter took a second to compose themselves, then reassembled, now standing side by side. They launched into what seemed to be a coordinated dance, featuring much swooping of arms and more leap-frogging. The rest of the attendees began wandering over to the dance floor, as they would a car crash.

"Is someone having a seizure?" a woman near Helen asked.

For the next half-hour, the funereal gathering became a party, with Peter and Gus at the center of it, performing a sequence of maneuvers loosely resembling square-dancing, then break-dancing, and frequently falling back on leap-frogging. Somehow their sweating, grinning, grimacing and frantic work convinced a few dozen couples to venture onto the dance floor.

Afterward, Peter and Gus found the folding chairs Helen had claimed earlier, and they asked for two gin and tonics each, and water, too, which Helen was happy to get from the bartender. When Helen visited her this second time, she saw her name, Terri, on a nametag stuck on her chest. The nametag hadn't been there before, Helen was sure, and now the highest button on Terri's shirt had been released, revealing an opulent curve of flesh, and a bit of underwire bra. Helen looked away, suddenly flushed.

"You with those two?" Terri asked.

Helen turned back to her, to that open and rosy face, and felt like she'd jumped in an ocean at sunrise. It was too much.

"My uncle and his friend," Helen said. "There's something wrong with them."

Terri watched the two men. Peter had his arm over the back of Gus's chair. Gus was leaning forward, massaging his knee.

"I guess at that age you can be less inhibited," Terri said.

As Terri looked at them, Helen allowed herself to look at Terri. Her eyes were dark and merry, her cheeks round and full.

"Weird thing is, I don't think they've had a drink yet," Helen said.

Terri laughed. She tilted her head, assessing Helen. "I like how you carry yourself," she said. "I have a friend your height who's always hunched over like a flamingo. But you own it."

If only you knew, Helen thought. An hour ago, I was hunched over, then my London uncle fixed me, citing Corinthian columns and Medea.

"I have a break in half an hour," Terri said, filling Helen's glass again. "Want to hang outside?"

When her break arrived, Helen was tipsy, and followed Terri to the bumper of her Subaru, where they vaped and laughed about Terri's ex, a career Marine with crippling anxiety and an edibles addiction. Helen told Terri far too much about her years of growing isolation, and all the while she knew she was saying too much, was painting a picture of herself as a pathetic shut-in who went to garlic events with her uncle. She stood up, feeling embarrassed.

"What time is it?" Helen asked. "Don't you have to be back soon?"

"Kiss me," Terri said, and in one fluid motion she grabbed Helen's shirt, pulled her down and kissed her with an open and ravenous mouth.

"That okay?" she asked.

Helen was stunned and wanted more. She leaned down and, with her hands behind her back—it seemed more polite, less presumptive—she kissed Terri longer, softer, grabbing at her lips with her teeth, briefly tasting red wine on her tongue. When they finished, Helen was gasping, half-blind. Her hands had found their way into Terri's shirt, under her bra, caught like rabbits under a fence.

Terri leaned away. "Gotta work," she said. "To be continued. Follow me home. I have a big shower." Then she hustled back into the Ramada, straightening her buttons.

Helen staggered inside and found Peter and Gus. They were placing fake bids on auction items—vacations in Kauai and Tahoe. "I'm taking the car," she said. "You guys can Uber. Don't ask questions. You owe me."

Helen drank water and coffee and felt sharp by the time Terri packed up the bar, started her Subaru, and waved for her to follow. She drove behind, watching Terri's taillights leave Gilroy proper and turn up into the San Gabriel foothills. All along Helen pictured herself pressed against Terri, her chest to her back, in Terri's big shower—all that water, everything so smooth.

But when Terri pulled into her ranch house driveway, her headlights swept over a crowd of teenagers, their silhouettes spidery, their shadows striping the yellow stucco.

Terri jumped out of her car and plowed through the crowd and into the house. Helen waited in her own car, on the street, watching teenagers lope off to their cars and bikes. After ten minutes, Terri hadn't emerged. Helen thought it through. The night was over. Terri had a kid, or more than one kid, and the kids—teenagers!— had thrown a party, thinking she'd be coming home later. Now they were arguing, and Terri was punishing them, and assessing damage, and clearing the house. There would be no big shower.

She texted Terri, saying she was leaving. Terri didn't answer. An hour later, after Helen was back in Tres Pinos, in bed, having masturbated twice, she got a response. *Sorry. Long story. Idiot daughter of mine.* A minute passed, then another ding. *They broke my parents' wedding plate.* Helen consoled her, they went to bed, and the next morning, just after dawn, Terri

texted again. *Have to be up in SF for a gig this week,
an old-timey costume thing, but see you when I get back?*

Peter was on Helen's futon again.

"It shouldn't be so hot here, not so close to
the coast," he said. He was wearing yellow tennis
shoes and salmon-colored shorts. He put his shoes
on the futon then took them off. He cracked his
knuckles and rubbed his eyes.

"Nope, shouldn't be so hot," he said.

"So did you guys work all those moves out
before, or…?" she asked.

"Nah, just spontaneous," Peter said. "Like
jazz." Then he was up like a leprechaun, suddenly
peering over her shoulder at her wall of proofs.

"No more parties," she said.

"I'm thinking no more Ramadas from now
on," he said. "We need something a bit classier."

"I'm done," Helen said.

"I like the costume ones," he said. He was pawing through the boxes at Helen's feet. "Ooh, look at this one!" he said, and picked up a stray invitation for a fundraiser for the Palace of Fine Arts in San Francisco. The Palace, a pseudo-Roman dome and collection of columns around a manmade pond, had been erected in haste in 1915, for the Panama-Pacific International Exposition—a kind of World Expo to celebrate the opening of the Panama Canal. It was the only part of the Expo that still remained, and it needed constant work to keep it standing.

"Those went out months ago," she said.

He continued reading from the invitation. "Orchestra. Dancing. Period-specific attire. And this is in three days! I'm going."

"You can't go," Helen said.

"It says you need to present the invite at the door. Is that a period-specific thing, too? That's perfect for us. You have more of these?"

"No," she said.

He laughed to himself. "You know, I actually have a top hat! From *My Fair Lady*."

"Where's Gus? Isn't Gus missing you? You should go work out more dance routines."

"Gus has Covid," Peter said. "Probably from Gilroy. He's actually pretty sick. He went to the hospital."

"Oh God, I'm sorry," Helen said. She really should never open her mouth; a very small percentage of the things she said were the right things to have said. The silence in the room stretched out.

Peter inhaled. "Yup, Gus got the Covid," he said.

"All the more reason to skip this one," Helen said. "Wait a month and then we can go to another event. For now, though, we need to cool it before someone notices. And you should be close to Gus. Does the hospital let you visit?"

Peter gave her a confused look. "He's not still *in* the hospital. I said he went *to* the hospital. But the line for testing there was too long, so he went home and did a rapid one."

"And he's positive?"

"Oh you know Gus, he's always upbeat."

Helen took a breath. Peter was near the door, and she thought of shoving him through.

"You'll wait this one out?" she asked.

"If you say so," he said.

After he was gone, Helen returned to the task she was in the middle of when he arrived: finding a costume for the 1915 party. She needed everything—corset, dress, shoes, parasol, fan. The event, partly outdoors, wasn't requiring masks, so she'd decided she needed casual face-coverings, diversions, anything to ensure some level of anonymity. She knew almost no one in San Francisco, so she was not too concerned with being discovered, but then again, all crime sprees ended when the criminals got sloppy.

Terri had not invited her to join her in the city, but Helen had done some cursory research and guessed that the old-timey party Helen mentioned was this Palace of Fine Arts thing. And she was feeling restless, reckless, not herself. The drive was only a few hours, and she wanted to see Terri again, wanted it to be weird and bold. She wanted to see what Terri looked like in one of those tight white shirts with the flowing sleeves and the high collars. Thinking about it, on the highway, was getting

Helen hot; she rolled down the window and thought about all the things she hadn't worked out, like where she was staying that night, when she'd go home, and what to do, how to live, if Terri, like Bartek, forgot her completely.

The event's website had promised a changing room where attendants would be available to contend with corsets and hoops, so Helen parked as close as she could to the Palace of Fine Arts— across the highway, near the beach, squeezed in a row of campers and windsurfers—and rushed to the building holding two garbage bags full of corsets and bustles. There were two women at the door, and Helen presented her invitation, the one Peter had inspected. It was the proof, and the only extra invitation printed. One of the young women accepted it, said, "Good luck," and directed Helen to the changing room.

The Palace of Fine Arts was a wide-open
space, round and the size of a small armory. The
women's changing area was indeed between
two basketball hoops, and there, at least forty
women were assembled, back to front, pulling
and grunting and laughing. The age range was
vast, from eighteen to seventy-five. About a
dozen women were in their twenties, their hair
coiled high, their necks exposed. The discomfort
was great, but the effect was transfixing. The
clothing flattered every body type, every face.
A woman of Helen's size and shape, but twenty
years older, approached her with kind eyes. She
was already dressed.

"You need help?"

Helen unpacked her corset and the woman
took it expertly in hand, fitting it carefully around
Helen's ribs. From there, the woman's hands were

quick and skilled. She pulled and threaded while humming softly to herself.

"Nothing left to tie," the woman finally said. "Is that your parasol?" she asked. "Indoors, at night, it's a stretch, but it's a lovely thing. I'm Barbara. Are you here alone?"

"I am," Helen said, thinking of Terri. Was she with Terri? She dropped the parasol and began nudging it under a nearby divan. "You?"

"I'm with my son," Barbara said. "You should meet him. He's stuck with me." The woman smiled while picking a strand of hair from Helen's sleeve. "Don't hold that against him. He's a normal person. If I see you out there, I'll introduce you."

Barbara squeezed her hand and strode off, her dress flowing, breathing beneath her like a living thing.

Helen found a free seat at one of the vanities and finished her makeup. She took cues from the other women around her, none of whom seemed quite sure if the colors should be demure or pronounced. Helen sat, looking at herself, bewildered. She was powdering her face, dressed like a turn-of-the-century heiress. What the fuck was she doing? Finished, she went outside, joining a trickle of partygoers making their way down a bending walkway. The strains of a small orchestra wafted from a doorway ahead, and at the entrance of a great hall, she paused. Sona really *could* be at this party. In fact, if she came to any party at all, it would be this one. Helen had brought a cloth mask, tucked into her sleeve. She put it on.

The hall was vast, alive with a hundred thousand lights. Chandeliers hung from the ceiling, which was covered in elaborate bunting

of violet and cream and gold to simulate sky and
clouds and god-light. The music was orchestral,
jaunty, of the era, Helen assumed, played by a
vast band in tuxedoes. A woman bassoonist with
cascading white hair was soloing. Helen roamed
through the room, looking for Terri. She skirted
the tables covered in white cloth, exuberant
arrangements of lilies and roses bursting from
each center. A woman in a blood-red costume
walked by, smelling strongly of lilac, to join two
friends in sunflower-yellow flapper dresses, and
an announcement came over that the orchestra
would be playing a composition written for
the 1915 fair. When the three women began
dancing, Helen was suddenly overcome. This is
glorious, Helen thought. So many parties were
just half-gestures toward merriment, but this was
something different. There was glee in the eyes

of everyone in the room, a sense that they were in the midst of something very odd, very ambitious, but which had been pulled off far beyond anyone's expectations. The effort and expense for all this, for one fleeting night, was obscene, and yet Helen felt that she would fight anyone who said it wasn't worth it.

The music stopped and a woman in a dress of the palest purple emerged, tapping her glass with a fork. "Now for some—gasp—organized fun," she said. "At an event like this, there would have been a number of group dances the attendees would have known. Which of course we do not know. But we happen to have a wonderful teacher who will familiarize us with a few of these dances. I promise you it will be painless." She first introduced the "Pan-Pacific One-Step," which required the two dancers to hold hands very high, over the shoulder, and then do a sort of Charleston with their legs. Two professional dancers demonstrated, then continued demonstrating while the rest of the attendees were urged to join them. A man next to Helen, about sixty and without hair anywhere—not on his head, not on his eyebrows—asked Helen if he might accompany her, and she was too startled to refuse. He was wearing white gloves.

They struggled through the number, his movements graceful but hers labored with the undercarriage and her hair, which was coming undone. She couldn't breathe, so took off her mask. No one, it seemed, was wearing masks anymore. He spun her, stepped on her toes and heels, apologizing each time, and finally, for the last half-minute, they were something like graceful. Afterward he thanked her and excused himself, joining a large throng of people his age at the bar.

Helen wandered the room, which began to feel smaller. From a distance she caught sight of a bartender who looked a bit like Terri, but older, with a high mound of white-gray hair. Could that be Terri in a wig? She investigated closer; it wasn't Terri. By then she'd visited every bar in the room, checked the face of every waitress, every place Terri might have been working, and she was nowhere.

And Helen had forgotten to eat. She was hungry, coming down from her champagne high, and very tired. She sat on a period-appropriate divan, under a fragrant fern, and glowered. She'd lost her mask, and felt exposed again. She'd driven two hundred miles for this, gotten dressed in this ludicrous way, chasing a woman based on the faintest clue.

"Everyone together!" a voice said. Helen knew this voice. She followed the sound to the foyer, where a group of women in black dresses were gathered, posing for a photo. Their dresses were identical, slinky black gowns with spaghetti straps, and when they all turned to their left, Helen finally understood. Madame X. The painting had been exhibited at the original Exposition, and now all the party's Mesdames X were taking a group photo. And just as the photographer counted down from three, an older man appeared in the frame, leaping from the wings, and that older man was Peter.

"Someone had to be John Singer Sargent!" he said, and after the Mesdames X laughed dutifully and shooed him away, his eyes met Helen's. He was wearing a tuxedo with tails, a high white collar, and a fake mustache. He looked utterly natural in it. His face was a radiant pink.

"Hi Hellie!" Peter said, utterly free of shame. "I didn't think you'd be here." He hugged her, smelling of cologne and cigars. He pulled back, surprised to see the fury in her eyes.

There were a few dozen people near, so she parsed her words. "I thought we agreed you weren't coming. To this. Or anything."

"Sure, but then I wanted to," he said brightly, and signaled to a waiter passing by with champagne. He took two flutes and gave one to Helen. "And I figured you weren't coming, so it wouldn't do any harm. Your main concern was my getting you in trouble, right? But if you weren't coming, then I couldn't get you in trouble."

The logic was unassailable, and she was angrier than before. "But how did you get in?"

"Gwen helped me," he said.

"Gwen?"

"Oh, I just remembered you two haven't met." He peered at the mass of Mesdames. "Gwen?"

One of the heads turned and a woman's huge brown eyes lit up. Peter pointed to Helen and mouthed her name, and Gwen came rushing over.

"I can't believe it!" she said, and pumped Helen's hand. "I didn't think you were coming. We finally meet! You're younger than I thought."

Helen was struck dumb. She stared at Gwen, with her long neck and delicate features. Gwen worked out of a converted barn; irrationally, Helen had always pictured her in overalls. But here she was with silky raven-black hair, dark eyes, and, next to her nostril, an astonishing mole.

"This is so messed up. Was this Peter's idea?" Helen asked.

"He got in touch, yes," Gwen said. "You know Gus has been sick, so—"

"How the hell do you know *Gus*?"

"Don't *you* know Gus?" Gwen asked.

"Yes, *I* know Gus!" Helen said, and a pair of elderly suffragettes looked their way. Helen lowered her voice. "What does Gus have to do with this?"

"Well," Gwen explained, "Gus really wanted to come to this event, given he's an amateur historian, and after he had that big Covid scare."

"He finally got into the hospital to do a real test," Peter explained.

"He didn't actually have Covid, thank god."

"But it was so sweet," Gwen continued, "how Peter said Gus really loved this era, and wanted to come up to the city and enjoy it all. I know it's unorthodox, Helen, but no one's being harmed, right? Here he is now."

It was Gus.

"Jesus Christ," Helen said.

He strode up in a burgundy suit and black top hat. Seeing Helen, he tipped it toward her and smiled broadly. It was the top hat from London.

"That's Peter's, I assume?" Helen said.

"How'd you know?" Gus said.

"If Sona's here," Helen said, "we're all fired."

"Sona's not here," Gwen said. "And she wouldn't fire us all. She definitely wouldn't fire Guillermo. She loves Guillermo."

"Not Guillermo," Helen said.

"You've never met him in person, right?" Gwen said, and hailed a tall man in an elaborately waxed beard.

"Guillermo, meet Helen," Gwen said.

Guillermo stretched his arms out for a hug, eyes closed. He was drunk. "Helen! Shit! Finally, all of us together! I can't believe—"

Helen wheeled toward Peter. "Was this you?"

"It was him!" Guillermo said. "It took your *uncle* to finally get us all together!"

Peter leaned toward Helen. "You look mad," he muttered.

"Don't you realize how stupid this is?" Helen roared. She pointed at her colleagues, one by one, like a scolding nun. "Sona *comes* to these events. She's probably somewhere with a headset and a clipboard. With every additional moron—and you're all just towering morons—you're exponentially increasing the chances we'll all get caught."

"Helen," Gwen said. "You really think she'd recognize any of us in period costumes, and half of us in masks?"

No one was wearing masks, but Helen was too angry to point this out. "Excuse me a second," she said, and pulled Peter down the hall, until they were out of earshot, under a kerosene lamp.

"Check out my monocle." He pulled a monocle from his front pocket and tried to secure it in his eye socket. "I only have eye for you," he said.

"You're an idiot," she said. "I could lose my job. We have to get everyone to leave." Helen thought desperate thoughts. She could pull a fire alarm. Did they have fire alarms in 1915? She wanted to smash Peter's head with the kerosene lamp.

"Helen. Helen," Peter said, taking both her hands in his. "Nothing matters right now. You know this. Sona knows this, too. We have another year, at least, before anything matters again."

"It does matter," Helen said. "It matters to me, now."

"No. It's an experiment right now," he said. "We're experimenting. We're emerging, and no one cares, and everyone understands." He squeezed her hands and smiled. His eyes were so old, so bright.

"I'm leaving," Helen said.

She walked the length of the glittering Palace and burst through the front doors. The sun had recently set and the sky was streaked with a garish pink. She wanted only to get into her car and drive home. She was halfway to the parking lot, in her corset and hoop dress, before she realized she'd forgotten her street clothes inside the Palace. She doubled back and stomped through the basketball court, where she found her clothes neatly bundled up and tucked under a divan, next to the parasol.

It had to have been Barbara. Oh, Barbara. Her kindness took Helen's legs. She had to sit down on the divan. Okay, she thought. People aren't all terrible. Now she just had to make it home.

She gathered her belongings and went back

into the night, the sky nearly black now, and crossed under the highway and rushed toward the beach, still in her hoop skirt and dress. She saw her car in the distance and was so grateful she laughed.

"This way, madame," a voice said.

A man in a gray tuxedo was suddenly in front of her, and with white-gloved hands was directing her to a colonnade of torches positioned on the beach. He seemed to be some kind of helper working the event.

"I'm heading home," she said. "Just getting my car."

"You know, you really should see this," the man said, abandoning all formality. "Fireworks start in a few minutes, and then they're doing a sort of sea battle on the bay. Lots of cannons and fake destruction. I saw the rehearsal earlier and it was bonkers."

Helen stood, breathing heavily. She really wanted to see all those things. She didn't want to start driving. The beach looked so calm. And there was probably a bar.

"See the cabana just over there?" the man asked. "That's for guests of the Pan-Pacific party. Get a drink and sit and watch the show."

It was so dark now that no one would see her, much less recognize her, not even Sona. So she tramped over to the cabana, where she found about thirty people dressed like her, and a lattice-work of overhead lights, and behind the bar, Terri. She was dressed in a snug white blouse, just as Helen had pictured and hoped for. Helen stopped breathing, watching Terri move, taking in her bright, cherubic face. Beyond, in the silver bay, two ships destined to fake-destroy each other were sailing slowly into place. Go, Helen told herself.

But she couldn't move. She could only think about going home.

Then the first cannon fired. The sound was a crack—almost an accidental crack—then an assertive boom. People gasped, laughed. Then the second ship fake-fired back—but god it seemed real, Helen thought—and soon the cannons were exchanging fire with abandon, white flashes illuminating the burgeoning gunsmoke. People clapped, screamed with delight. It was madness, totally unnecessary and reckless in every way. And because the aural plane had been busted open, and people were shrieking approvingly at a feigned sea battle full of fire and the delightful memory of bodies blown apart, Helen thought, Well, shit. She felt suddenly feral and free, so walked quickly, directly up to Terri's bar, snuck up behind her, put her hands on her hips and said, "Hey bartender."

Terri spun and swept her eyes all over Helen—
her hair, dress, shoes, eyes again, lips. She threw
her arms around Helen and squeezed her with
bewildering strength, and Helen was so grateful
to have left her house. There were so many things
outside the house. Fuck my house, she thought.
Over Terri's shoulder, the ship-battle continued,
the cannons sounding, the smoke rising, fire
overtaking one ship's ghostly sails.

"How did you know I was here?" Terri asked.

"I didn't," Helen said. "I just had an
invitation."

"Oh god, I'm hyperventilating," Terri said.
"You look gorgeous." She grabbed Helen's lower
back and pulled her close, and their mouths took
each other, lunged tongues and tasted each other,
swallowed worlds and ended time. Finally Terri
pulled away and composed herself. "So will you

stay here with me? Pretend to bartend. Stay for the fireworks! Can you stay with me out here? It's not too weird?"

"No, no, no, no," Helen said. "I can definitely stay. I want to stay out here. I'm staying."

DAVE EGGERS's recent books include *The Eyes & the Impossible* and *The Every*.

ACKNOWLEDGMENTS

Thanks first and foremost to Tessa and Eve, who asked a very good question. Thanks also to these people who helped bring this book into the world: Amanda Uhle, Ed Park, Amy Sumerton, Stephanie Pierson, Justin Carder, and Angel Chang. Particular thanks go to Hannah Tinti, an extraordinary editor who, with her team at *One Story*, helped this story immeasurably.

All proceeds from this book go to McSweeney's, a nonprofit publishing company in San Francisco that for twenty-five years has sought to find and amplify new voices.